Blake Canter

THE ROYAL RACCOON

Cathy Bellows

T 2152

Macmillan Publishing Company
New York

Collier Macmillan Publishers
London

For my mother and father

Macmillan Publishing Company
866 Third Avenue, New York, NY 10022
Collier Macmillan Canada, Inc.
Printed and bound in Singapore
First American Edition

10 9 8 7 6 5 4 3 2 1

The text of this book is set in 16 point Horley Old Style.
The illustrations are rendered in watercolor.

Library of Congress Cataloging-in-Publication Data
Bellows, Cathy.
The royal raccoon/Cathy Bellows.—1st American ed.
p.   cm.
Summary: Frederick, a snobbish raccoon and self-proclaimed prince
of the garbage dump, discovers the value of friendship when two
ferocious dogs drive him out of his palace and into the swamp home
of three wild raccoons.
ISBN 0-02-709031-0
1. Raccoons—Fiction. 2. Friendship—Fiction.
3. Swamps—Fiction. I. Title.
PZ7.B4195Ro   1989   [E]—dc19   88-8282   CIP   AC

Fred was no ordinary raccoon.
Fred was rich. He was filthy rich!
He lived in a dump filled with garbage. And all the trash, and all the rubbish, and all the junk belonged to him. Everything was his.

He had a magnificent palace made out of old
cardboard boxes, and a cozy bed filled with crinkly
newspapers. There was a big bathtub to swim in, and
rubber duckies to play with; and every day, rain or shine,
a dump truck arrived with all kinds of tasty treats to eat.
Pizza crust, wallpaper, potato chips—Fred had it all!

What a kingdom! thought Fred as he gazed across his junkyard. I must be the richest, the noblest, the best-dressed raccoon in the whole world! And that is why he decided to call himself Prince Frederick Bottlecap Macaroni III. It was the longest, grandest—not to mention tastiest—name he could think of.

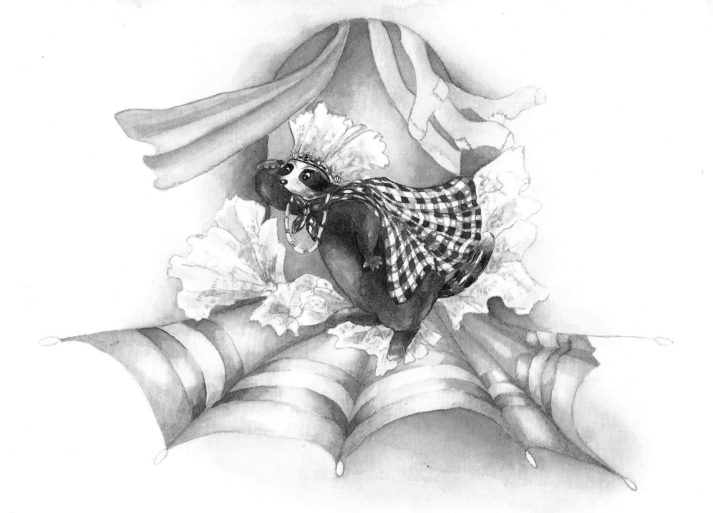

But one morning Prince Frederick awoke to the sound
of barking.

"Who goes there?" he yelled, standing atop his palace.
"Who dares enter my kingdom?" Not far away, among
the mattress springs and old tires, stood two very
ferocious dogs.

"How dare you come here?" he shouted. "Off with
you! Out of my dump!"

But the dogs liked the dump so much, they decided to stay. So they barked and howled and chased the poor raccoon out of his palace, past his tub, through the tires, and into the wild swamp beyond.

"Ruffians!" cried the raccoon as he climbed up a tree and hid high in the branches.

"We're taking over this dump!" barked the dogs. "So stay out, raccoon, and don't come back!" Then, laughing and howling, they marched back to their new kingdom.

"I'm ruined," cried Prince Frederick, wringing his paws. "My palace, my tub—my whole kingdom is gone, and worst of all, I miss my rubber duckies." The poor raccoon was so miserable, he began to weep. "What's to become of me?" he wailed. "I'm all alone in this wild place. I'm stuck in a swamp!"

But he wasn't exactly alone, for in the branches he noticed three wild and scruffy raccoons grinning at him.

"Don't worry about a thing," said the first raccoon. "You can come and live with us in the swamp. My name's Daisy, and this is Woody, and this is Fern. Why, in no time at all, you'll be just as wild and scruffy as we are!"

"Me? Wild? I've never heard of such an awful idea. Prince Frederick Bottlecap Macaroni III could never be wild. I'm royal, and I'm used to a kingdom of my own!"

But Prince Frederick was beginning to get hungry. So he decided to see what those wild raccoons could do.

"Very well," he declared. "You scruffy ones may bring me my lunch. Pizza crust, potato chips, wallpaper—I'm not fussy. Anything the garbage truck brings will do."

"There's no garbage truck here!" cried Fern. "But follow us, Freddy. We'll find you something good to eat." And into the swamp they disappeared.

Well, never had Prince Frederick walked so far just to get some lunch. He climbed through bushes, and ducked under branches, and got scratched by all kinds of nasty twigs, till finally the wild raccoons came upon an ant hill.

"How about some juicy bugs?" said Woody.

"Are you kidding?" said the Prince. "Royalty doesn't eat bugs!"

So they searched a little farther, till they found some yummy roots. "Roots are always good for the teeth!"

But the Prince shook his head. "Roots? Never!"

On and on they went, till they came to a forest of ferns. "Here's something you're sure to like," they cried. "Fiddlehead ferns! They're our favorites!"

Prince Frederick took a sniff, then he took a nibble, and then he spit it out. "Horrors!" he cried. "These are weeds!"

By now he was beginning to feel rather dusty. So he decided to give some more orders. "Show me to my bath!" he demanded. "I want to take a dip!"

"Sure thing, Freddy," said the wild raccoons, and skipping and scampering, they took the little prince deeper and deeper into the swamp, till they came to a large pond.

What a lovely pond it was! Bright water lilies covered the water, and pretty birds stood squawking along the edge. Daisy, Woody, and Fern dove right in.

This is a very strange bathtub, thought the Prince, and when he dipped his toe in the water, he let out a scream.

"This water's cold!" he cried. "And what's more, there's mud at the bottom of this tub! How dare you bring me to a mudhole? I demand to see my palace! This has been a very bad day, and your Prince needs a nap!"

The wild raccoons took Freddy even deeper into the swamp, till they came to a tall pine tree.

"This is where we sleep," they said proudly, pointing to their tree house. "And because you're new, we'll let you have the softest, thickest branch in the whole tree!"

"Branch! You expect the Prince of the Dump to sleep on a branch, with no newspapers, no pillows, no little blankie?"

But the little prince was so tired and so upset with all that had happened, that he climbed up the tall tree and stretched out on the thick branch.

Maybe this is a bad dream, he thought. Maybe I'll close my eyes . . . and when I open them, I'll be back in my dump. So he squeezed his eyes shut.

When Freddy opened his eyes, there on the branch above him were seven little possums hanging upside down by their tails.

"Hello, Mr. Raccoon," they squeaked. "We're your neighbors! Isn't it wonderful? We live in the branch just above yours!"

"That does it!" said the raccoon. "I've had it! Being wild is not for me! I'm leaving!" And down the tree he climbed.

"Where are you going?" asked the wild raccoons.

"Home!" said the Prince. "I'm going back to my dump, and if I can't go there, I'll find another dump, and if I can't find another dump, I'll live in a garbage can. But I'm not staying in this wild swamp. It's no place for a prince like me!" And into the swamp he stomped.

"Oh, you mustn't!" cried the wild raccoons. "Please, Freddy, it's dangerous out there!" But when they tried to stop him, the little prince shooed them away.

Through the thick forest he marched, stumbling and grumbling and waving his arms all about. He trudged through ferns and tramped over bushes, till finally he came to a great marsh of tall reeds. And there in the warm mud lay a big old alligator, fast asleep.

At least the Prince thought he was asleep. But when he tried to tiptoe by, the gator opened one eye and said, "Where are you off to, young raccoon? Don't you know it's dangerous in this marsh? Why, you never know who may be lurking in these reeds."

"I happen to be looking for a dump," said the Prince. "You see, I'm a prince, and I must have a new kingdom."

"I knew it!" said the gator, opening both eyes. "I knew, the minute I saw you, that you were royalty." Then he bowed his head and said, "Your Royal Highness, let me introduce myself. I am Duke La Chomp, at your service."

"Duke?" said the Prince, and he took a closer look at the big green gator. "Well, if you're a duke, perhaps you could direct me to the nearest dump. I simply must get out of this mucky old swamp."

"A prince in a swamp? Why, the very idea!" said the gator. "Please, Your Majesty, I know a wonderful dump, perfect for a royal raccoon like yourself. Please, I beg you, climb on my back and let me take you there."

So the little raccoon sat down on the big gator's back, and through the muddy waters they swam.

Farther and farther into the swamp they went. As he paddled along, the gator's grin grew bigger and wider and toothier and toothier. What a lucky gator I am! he thought, and his huge mouth began to water.

Finally they came to the deepest, darkest part of the swamp, to the place where nobody but alligators dared to go, because it was so deeply creepy and scary. And there, in the midst of a thick black bog filled with rotten old cypress trees, the great gator stopped.

"Why are we stopping here, Duke?" asked the prince. "This doesn't look like a very nice dump to me."

"This is no dump!" said the gator as he headed toward the biggest, oldest, most rotten tree of all. "This is my home." And inside the hollow tree trunk he slithered.

Now the little raccoon was beginning to get awfully nervous, especially when the Duke set him on a plate and sprinkled salt on his head.

"You know," said Fred, "I don't believe you're a duke at all. I think you're just a plain ordinary reptile!"

"Well, I don't think you're a prince at all," said the gator. "I think you're just a plain ordinary supper!" Then he grabbed Fred by the tail and opened his jaws wide.

"Help!" cried the poor raccoon as he dangled above those spiky alligator teeth. "Please! Somebody help me!"

Just as the gator was about to chomp, through the door came the wild raccoons.

"Let go of our Freddy!" they cried, grabbing the gator by the tail.

"Let go of my tail!" growled the gator.

"Let go of *my* tail!" screamed Freddy.

And with all that pushing and pulling and hooting and hollering, the big old tree began to shake and tremble. It swayed this way and that, weeping and creaking, till finally it cracked! Into the water it crashed, where it sank—*plunk*—down to the bottom of the thick black bog.

"My house!" cried the gator as they tumbled into the water. "You've ruined my beautiful rotten house!" But by the time he surfaced and looked around, all the raccoons were gone.

Across the bog the raccoons scurried. Faster and faster they ran, through the reeds and under the trees and all around the bushes and ferns. And through it all, no one ran faster, no one jumped higher, no one leaped farther than little Prince Frederick. He ran and he ran and he didn't stop until he reached the old pine tree.

"What a place this wild swamp is!" he cried as the sun began to rise. "What a terrible, wonderful place! That alligator was so terrible, and you raccoons were so wonderful! Oh, please, Daisy, please, Woody, let me stay here with you. Please, Fern, say I can stay!"

Well, the wild raccoons could hardly believe their ears.

"Don't you want to go back to your dump kingdom?" asked Daisy. "Back to your pizza crusts and rubber duckies and bed of crinkly newspapers?"

"Certainly not!" said Frederick. "What kind of a place is that for a raccoon? No, I want to be where my friends are! I want to be brave and loyal and scruffy, just like you!"

So, Prince Frederick Bottlecap Macaroni III changed his name to Fred Fiddlehead, and he stayed in the swamp, where he lived wildly ever after.

155